WORD BIRD
MAKES WORDS WITH HEN

by Jane Belk Moncure
illustrated by Linda Hohag

THE CHILD'S WORLD

MANKATO, MN 56001

We acknowledge with gratitude the review of the Word Bird Short Vowel Adventure *books by Dr. John Mize, Director of Reading, Alamance County Schools, Graham, North Carolina.*

—The Child's World

Library of Congress Cataloging in Publication Data

Moncure, Jane Belk.
  Word Bird makes words with Hen.
  — A short "e" adventure.

  (Word Bird's short vowel adventures)
  Summary: When his father brings him some new word puzzles, Word Bird makes up more words with his friend Hen. Each word that they make up leads them into a new activity.
  [1. Vocabulary. 2. Birds—Fiction. 3. Chickens—Fiction] I. Hohag, Linda, ill. II. Title.
III. Series: Moncure, Jane Belk.   Word Bird's short vowel adventures.
PZ7.M739Wnh 1984   [E]   83-23944
ISBN 0-89565-260-9 -1991 Edition

WORD BIRD
MAKES WORDS WITH HEN

One day Papa came
home with some new
word puzzles.

"Do you like word puzzles?" asked Papa.

"You bet," said Word Bird.

Word Bird put

with

What did Word Bird make?

Word Bird counted to
ten... and back again.
Can you?

Then Word Bird put

p with en

What word did he make?

p en

"I can write words
with a pen," he said.
"I can write ten."

And he did.

Then Word Bird put

h with en

What word did he make?

h en

Just then, Word Bird's friend, Hen, came to play.

"Hi, Hen."

"I can put word puzzles together," said Hen. She put

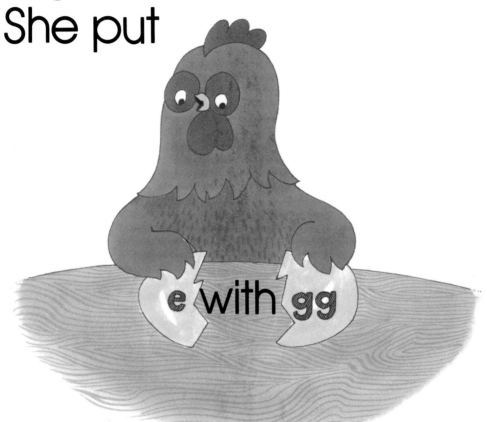

e with gg

What word did Hen make?

e gg

"Let's make an Easter
egg tree," said Word Bird.

It was a nice egg tree.
But they made a mess.

Mama said, "Please
clean up this mess."
And they did.

Then Word Bird made another word. He put

j with et

What word did he make?

j et

"Let's go for a jet ride," said Word Bird.

And they did.

Then Hen put

ch with est

What word did Hen make?

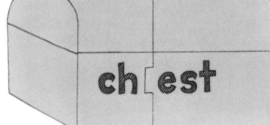

ch est

"Let's see what is in this chest," said Word Bird.

The chest was full of
shells—seashells.

"Let's play with the
shells," said Word Bird.

They made a mess!
What did Mama say?

"I will make another word," said Word Bird. He put

What word did he make?

"I have a tent," said
Word Bird.

"Let's play in your tent,"
said Hen. And they did.

They played in the
tent until ten o'clock.

Later it began to snow.
"I will make another word,"
said Word Bird.

He put

sl with ed

What word did he make?

sl ed

"I have a sled," said
Word Bird.

"Let's get on the sled,"
Hen said.

They went down the hill
on the sled ten times.

Then Mama called,
"Come in, Word Bird."

Mama said, "Look at
your face!"

Word Bird looked in
the mirror. He saw RED!

You can read more word
puzzles with

p et

s et

g et

n et

d en

m en

b ell

s ell

f ell

t ell

p ep

st ep

Now you make some word puzzles.